Written by Julie Labossiere

Illustrated by Dwayne Brown

We would like to thank Laura
for helping to make this book happen!

Getting ready for the day, Amy thought about all the lessons her surf coach, Kirk, had taught her about surfing. All the lessons to prepare her for today, as today would be the first time she went out to surf without Kirk by her side. She was scared that she would not remember what to do without Kirk there with her.

Soon after, she was sitting on the beach waiting for Kirk to arrive. Her brother, sister and cousin were all there with her. Amy grew up watching them all surf and thought it looked fun. She already knew how to swim so she thought it would be simple to learn to surf.

Today, they were there to watch Amy. While she waited, Stephanie, Aaron and Frank were off tossing a Frisbee back and forth.

It was a perfect day to be at the beach. The weather was just right with the sun shining, blue skies and a light breeze. The waves were coming in a couple of minutes apart. As Amy watched the waves coming in, she remembered some of the basic rules to surfing that Kirk had told her.

"Be patient," Kirk would tell her. "The perfect wave may not be the first one you see. You may have to wait a few minutes, but you'll know the right wave when you see it coming."

"How will I know?" she had asked.

"You'll just know," he said.

Today would be the first time Kirk wouldn't be with her to point out the perfect wave. She hoped she wouldn't have to wait too long.

Surfing was not what Amy expected it to be. She thought it would have been easier to learn but she had to take lessons with Kirk and she practiced a lot.

Kirk taught Amy how to paddle on the surf board, how to balance on the board, and then how to get up on the board and balance in the water.

Eventually she was able to put it all together and practice in the deep water. She fell off the board a lot but the more she practiced, the better she became at it. She actually even surfed a couple of times with Kirk's help.

Just then, she heard Kirk's car door shut behind her. She turned and watched him grab his own surf board from the top of his car and walk over to her on the beach.

"Are you ready?" he asked as he stood his board in the sand and sat next to Amy.

"I think so. I'm just nervous," she told him. She took a deep breath and watched as she moved the sand from side to side with her feet.

"I know you are but you have been practicing for weeks. From what I have seen, I know you are ready. I will still be here with you, just watching from the beach this time instead of being out there with you. This will show me that you remember what I taught you. Remember- patience, speed and balance."

"Got it," she told him. "Here I go!"

Amy took a deep breath, picked her board up out of the sand and started running towards the water.

"I know how to surf. I've been doing it almost everyday with Kirk. I can do this," she told herself. She started running into the water and then laid the surf board down and began paddling out to the deeper waters.

When she felt she was far enough out in the water she got up and sat on her board and looked out to the deeper water for the start of a new wave.

A minute later she saw a new wave approaching.

"That's not it," she said to herself. She let that wave roll under her and she waited for the next one to start.

A few minutes later, after Amy let a few waves pass, she was ready to take a wave and saw a new one starting to roll her way.

"This is it!" she thought. She started paddling towards the shore to gain speed so she could keep up with the wave. It quickly approached and as it started to roll up under her she jumped up to stand on her board and began to gain control and balance.

Her board was gliding along the water as the wave grew up out of the water and started to round up over her head. Riding out of the tunnel that the wave created around her, she was standing on her board and she couldn't help but smile as she was surfing!

She was so happy that she was actually surfing that she reached out and touched the wave around her as she glided through it just to make sure it was real.

What felt like seconds later, the wave began to crash and fade onto the shore. As Amy's board reached the end of the wave, she jumped off and dragged her board onto the shore where Kirk and her family were cheering for her. They all greeted her with hugs and excitement.

"Well, I think you can officially call yourself a surfer," Kirk told her with a smile.

She did it! She was so proud of herself.

Amy was ready to go back for more and she did along with her brother, sister, cousin and Kirk. They surfed until it was time to go home.

That night, Amy felt like she could do anything she wanted with a little practice and patience. So she started to think of what she could learn next as she dozed off.

Amy's Adventures

Follow Amy in all her adventures!

Facebook Page: Amy's Adventures
Website: amysadventurebooks.com

Made in the USA
Lexington, KY
25 September 2012